Drummond Welburn

Tales of Early Love

To sweethearts, wife, mother, native land, church, God

Drummond Welburn

Tales of Early Love
To sweethearts, wife, mother, native land, church, God

ISBN/EAN: 9783337343682

Printed in Europe, USA, Canada, Australia, Japan

Cover: Foto ©Andreas Hilbeck / pixelio.de

More available books at **www.hansebooks.com**

TALES OF EARLY LOVE

To
Sweethearts,
Wife,
Mother,
Native Land,
Church,
God.

TO

SWEETHEARTS, WIFE, MOTHER, NATIVE LAND, CHURCH, GOD.

—

BY A TENNESSEEAN.

—

MOST RESPECTFULLY DEDICATED TO THE
MISSES B., OF NEW YORK CITY.

—

PRINTED FOR THE AUTHOR.
PUBLISHING HOUSE OF THE M. E. CHURCH, SOUTH.
BARBEE & SMITH, AGENTS, NASHVILLE, TENN.
1892.

EMELINE SKATING ON THE DELAWARE RIVER.

(2)

SARAH AT HOME.

TALES OF EARLY LOVE.

Hail, holy love! thou word that sums all bliss,
That fills the bowl and banquet of the sky—
The sparkling cream of all time's blessedness.

YOUNG ladies, I have come to share your smiles
And catch the sweet contagion of your joy.
Your prankish plays shall make me young again,
Call back the romance of departed years;
When your grandmothers, in their youthful bloom,
Could fascinate and charm the coldest hearts.
You ask for tales of glad, unselfish love,
When nature's springtime strewed with fragrant flow'rs
The pathway trodden by light, buoyant steps.
You say that I in the bright days of old
Laid votive off'rings upon love's pure shrine.
Yes, ladies, I have ever been in love
With some fair daughter of majestic Eve.

My mother, left a widow in her prime,
Pressed to her bosom her loved orphan child;
And as I upward gazed into her eyes,
Taught me to love all of the gentle sex.
Through nearly fourscore years I've longed to feel
The loving pressure of her arms again.
Pardon an old man's freely flowing tears:
She'll soon embrace me in God's paradise.

.   .   .   .

But you would have me tell a joyous tale
Of youth's devotion to some winsome lass.
A Sabbath morning threw its sacred charm
Around the inmates of our humble home;
The air was perfumed with delightsome scents
Of honeysuckles, roses, pinks, and balm,
Rising like incense toward the throne of God;

(4)

Industrious bees and flitting humming birds
Drew from the flow'rs richer delicious drafts
Than fabled nectar of false, fabled gods.
I had been told of my good uncle's home,
Two miles away lifting its lofty roof,

My mother, most demurely reverent.

And now the longed for day of days had come
When I should visit that enchanting place.
All neatly washed and decked in Sunday clothes,
We passed the orchard gayly blossoming,

Until a flaming redbird crossed our path.

(6)

Across the narrow bay of Chincoteague.

The hick'ry trees, in their green garniture,
"The oaks, majestic monarchs of the woods,"
In grandeur throned through hoary centuries.
We crossed the rippling brook, walked up the slope,
And through the thicket of quite recent growth.
I gazed in wonder upon old Fort Hill,
Where cannon thundered in the time of war
To drive marauding Britons to their ships;
And thus far kept within the well-trod path.
My mother, most demurely reverent,
Talked much of God, who painted the fair flow'rs
And breathed their fragrance lavishly around;
Of Christ, who died that sinners might be saved,
Who e'en would help a little boy be good.
But I was chasing modest "Jennie Wren,"
Or list'ning to a robin's cheerful song;
Until a flaming redbird crossed my path,
And drew me where the pines were whispering
To breezes playing with their lofty tops,
While ocean's deepest bass fell on my ear.
On the smooth carpet of the wooded plain,
Woven of needly shatters of the pine,
I slipped and fell, but rose again, to gaze,
Through glades that opened eastward toward the sea,
On the most grand, magnificent of scenes.
Across the narrow bay of Chincoteague
Two islands stood apart, as if to form
An inlet and protection for the fleets
Of coast wise commerce near that favored shore.
I saw the piney curtains of the beach
Drawn back on either side, to open up
To human view old ocean's majesty.
With awe-struck spirit I had seen the sky,
By day and night, in its immensity:
Its sparkling stars, its mildly beaming moon,
Its drifting clouds, and its bright, dazzling sun.
Its distances seemed to forbid approach;
But the broad, boundless ocean at my feet
Not only with its vastness awed my soul.
Its large ships sailing to mysterious ports
Held my imagination as entranced.

The luster of the wide-spread satin sails
Made of me a Columbus for a time,
Longing to visit the most distant coasts,
And claim their startling grandeur as my own.
My musings ended with my morning walk,
And my good uncle's hospitable home
Threw wide its doors to welcome honored guests.
My aunt and my tall cousins kissed the boy,
Who, less than five years old, stood bashfully
Until the master of the mansion came,
Saw his dead brother's image in his child,
And held him to his palpitating heart,
Dropping the tears of age on childhood's cheek.
'Tis wonderful how much the young can learn
In one brief, fleeting hour of early life!
Insects and birds, sweet flow'rs and tow'ring trees
The ocean's grandeur and the concave sky,
Voices of kindred, clasps of friendly hands,
Religion's counsels and inspiring hopes—
All ministered to one expanding mind.
But a mere child, months younger than myself,
Gave the impressive lesson of that hour,
Taught the great mystery of youthful love.
My Cousin Margaret, a sprightly girl,
Came in to entertain the little boy.
The lily' and the rose could not compare
With the clear colors of her dimpled cheeks;
Nor apple blossoms, waving in the wind,
With the rich hues of her fair countenance.
Her features seemed the work of God's own hand,
And holy angels might have left their thrones
To print fond kisses on her glowing lips.
Nor sky, nor ocean, nor the shining sun
Could match the blue and brightness of her eyes.
Her form was symmetry, her motions grace;
Her ev'ry movement kindled new delight;
Her voice was more than music to my ear,
Such tones were hers as heav'n might stoop to hear;
They seemed to wing the happy hours away.
The pleasures of that day are with me still.
They bring to memory most pure delight,

And give to age the charm of childhood's dreams.
But, ladies, you have listened patiently,
To a rude rhapsody of other days.

You say: "Go on."   Well, I will then proceed.
I would not talk like "Ovid" if I could,

My Cousin Margaret, a sprightly girl,
Came in to entertain the little boy.

Nor speak such burning words as Byron wrote;
I cannot tell of love like Burns or Scott,
Nor Campbell of a "rapture-smitten frame,"
Or Eden's joyless wild "till woman smiled;"
Nor love's own poet, brilliant Thomas Moore.

But you shall have a tale of village life,
When that grand classic, Webster's spelling book,
Taught the wise tactics of a warfare waged
Over the spelling of our English words.
Whole ranks went down before our bold attacks,
Brave victors triumphed in great battles won.

When that grand classic, Webster's spelling book,
Taught the wise tactics of a warfare waged
Over the spelling of our English words.

I was a young Napoleon in those fights,
And when "the sun of Austerlitz" was seen
I by shrewd signs, and whispers slyly breathed,
Kept my fair Josephine crowned near my throne.
She was most lovely. Six short years ago
I saw her grandchild, wearing her sweet smiles,

And loved her much for her grandmother's sake,
Who in the twenties, sixty years before,
Had won the love of my devoted heart,
When, without cruelty to fleecy flocks,
Boys threw sheep's eyes at girls they fondly loved.
You smile at the simplicity of age;

When, without cruelty to fleecy flocks,
Boys threw sheep's eyes at girls they fondly loved.

Yet life's sublimest joyousness oft springs
From unsuspected bliss in simplest things.

You say: "Proceed." Esther, a Quakeress,
With saintly features, won me at sixteen.
I loved the drab-dressed people for her sake,
And "thees" and "thous" seemed heaven's choicest words.
I went to Quaker meeting, and enjoyed

Esther, a Quakeress,
With saintly features, won me at sixteen.

(13)

The silent service, gazing on her face.
She was far fairer than a poet's dream
Of all that's beautiful in earth or sky.
Milton's grand Eve, by Dubufe's pencil drawn,
Had no such blonde perfection as she wore,
Lacking the charm of living magnetism,
That neither words nor colors can portray.
Her looks were sermons that, rebuking sin,
Made men feel penitent for loving her.
I guess she goes to Quaker meetings yet,
Perhaps discourses, and says "thee" and "thou"
To reverential hundreds of good friends.

. . . .

When I was next enamored, Emeline
Was tall and stately, dignified, refined,
Majestic as Zenobia, and as proud.
She had known happier days, but fortune frowned,
And she descended to the lowly place
Of clerk to a confectioner, and sold
Delicious *morceaux* to admiring crowds.
Demure and grave, she stood with soft white hands,
To deal out sweets less sweet than her sweet self
Seeming unconscious of the hungry eyes
That feasted on the beauty they beheld.
Her black hair curled upon her snowy brow,
And dimpled cheeks with fitful blushes flushed,
Her dark bright eyes looked out upon the world
With a most lofty and disdainful gaze,
Until her lovers gladly would have paid
To have some artist paint upon her face
A smile to light its glorious loveliness.
But she smiled not upon the multitudes.
At church and on the street she wore a veil
To hide her features from intrusive eyes.
'Twas said her smiles were kept for one who loved
The haughty beauty in her early days,
And promised to restore prosperity,
And then enthrone her in his heart and home.
I much regret that I could never learn
How much she prospered in her later years,
Nor how she lavished smiles upon one man.

But you grow weary of these tales of love
And those fair, beauteous girls of bygone days;
Let your sweet voices entertain us now.

You still demand "an old man's memories
Of former times, when youth and love still reigned."

Demure and grave, she stood with soft white hands,
To deal out sweets less sweet than her sweet self.

I'll tell of Sarah: how she walked to school,
And passed my place of business day by day.
The large poke bonnet which at first she wore,
Made of drab fur, decked with an ostrich plume,
Trimmed with wide ribbon of a peach bloom hue,
Told of her coming quite a square away.
I've watched through window panes till in the snow

SARAH IN SUMMER.

She was a customer, and oft detained
To look at many things she did not want.

Her fairy footsteps could be plainly seen,
And glimpses of her features could be gained
In spite of envious ribbons, flow'rs, and furs.
She was a customer, and oft detained
To look at many things she did not want;
And then called back to take from my own hand
Bright boxes, pictures, and gay ornaments
With which fine goods were tastefully adorned.
On Saturdays, when she could be at home,
I to her mother took light merchandise,
That she might the most beautiful select
Ere other eyes had looked upon their hues,
And I might gaze on her fair daughter's face.
We never talked of love, but to our ears
The servants of two households, gossiping,
Told of the love each to the other bore.
From twelve to twenty she was all my own,
And I was hers despite fair Esther's bloom
Or all the grandeur of proud Emeline.
She was the last loved object that I laid
On God's pure altar·when his ministry
Demanded my poor heart with all its pow'rs.
Years after, when we both had long grown old,
And children's children stood around our knees,
I trod the walks made sacred by her steps,
Nor stopped until her father's dwelling house
Became the Mecca of my pilgrimage.
I thought upon the Sabbaths when I sat
Through the long prayer book service for her sake,
And wished it longer, that my eyes might feast
Upon her beauty through protracted hours.
I strolled away to the old ivied church,
So dear to her that I so long had loved,
And dared to hope that with the glorified,
Freed from all earthly taint, we'll meet again,
And pure-like angels, ever live, and love.

.   .   .   .

Years passed, self-doomed to cold celibacy,
When I would not permit myself to see
Bewitching features or enchanting smiles;
2

SARAH AT HOME.

On Saturdays, when she could be at home,
I to her mother took light merchandise
That I might gaze on her fair daughter's face.

I trod the walks made sacred by her steps.

(19)

But nature would sometimes assert her pow'r,
And show such loveliness to human eyes
As captivated the most stoical,
In spite of resolutions or of rules.

Anna, a Presbyterian, came to hear
The preaching of a zealous Methodist;

With all the glory the old masters gave
To holy Mary in mediæval times.

And, innocent of wrong to any one,
Led captive the young preacher's truant heart.
Intelligent, refined, genteel, devout, ·
Her saintly countenance, Madonnalike,
Had all the glory the old masters gave
To holy Mary in mediæval times.

Rosa, with pinklike features, form and frame,
Fair, fragile blossom, caught my youthful eye.

(21)

Devotion beamed as brightly in her face
As if she never thought of aught but heav'n.
I sought no introduction to the maid,
But that bright vision haunted me for years.
I saw her when she brought grown children out
To hear me preach. She still was beautiful,
With the old heav'nly glory on her face.

Rosa, with pinklike features, form and frame,
Fair, fragile blossom, caught my youthful eye.
She seemed to need protection from the world,
Such as a man's strong heart longed to extend.
Besides, she was the champion of my Church,
Defending it against its enemies
With words of wisdom far beyond her years
And the resistless pow'r of a pure life.
The elements of martyrdom in her
Lacked only flames for full development.
She threw her loving smile upon my path,
And rode through wintry storms to hear me preach.
Her friends were told how dear I was to her.
She chose the school that I did recommend,
And let me know that I might find her there.
She was too young to marry, so was I—
At least the Churches said they knew I was—
So we proposed to wait through the slow years,
Until our youthful minds were more mature.
Her parents did not smile upon my suit;
They willed that she should wed some wealthy man,
Which to the world would seem most wise in them.
I must teach disobedience to a child,
And steal her from her teachers if I could,
And rashly marry ere I was prepared,
Or risk home influence to part loving hearts.
So I informed her I would still be hers,
To wait most patiently while she desired,
And said that earth and hell in vain might try
To part me from her, against her own will.
Her parents had their way, and months rolled on,
Time cured our troubles and released our hearts
From the sweet thraldom that had held them fast.

I was well married, Rosa soon was wed
To one entirely worthy of her heart,
And in three years she gently slept in death.

The elements of martyrdom in her
Lacked only flames for full development.

Now, ladies, you'll excuse your aged friend,
And let your own sweet voices charm our ears.
You say, "No, no;" and claim another tale
Of youthful love to entertain the hour.

But what if that should bring me too near home,
And give most grave offense to one whose love
In "rosy bondage long has held my heart?"
You still insist that I shall take all risks,
And talk right on about most sacred ties.

'Twas Sunday night when, rising from my knees,
I saw the paragon of human kind.

A new appointment claimed my services,
Taxed all my energies, and brought strange crowds
To witness a young man's embarrassment.
'Twas Sunday night when, rising from my knees,
I saw the paragon of human kind.

I knew she had not just dropped down from heav'n,
But where on earth had such perfection grown?
She sung in tones I never heard before;
Her voice came grandly, sweetly through the sounds
Upraised by others in the praise of God,
As if some seraph from th' eternal throne
Had brought to earth the music of the skies.
My sermon was to other ears addressed;
I could command no language fit for hers.
On Thursday night her sister and herself
Brought their certificates to join my Church.
I clasped a hand too pure for man to touch;
It sent a heav'nly thrill to my rapt heart.
Her name, with trembling hand placed on my book,
Cast its bright radiance over the whole page.
Through twelve months we were often face to face,
While rosy blushes flushed our glowing cheeks.
Too sacred far she seemed for wedded life,
I did not dare to hope she might be mine;
And so we took no time for lovers' talk.
Indeed, so fascinating was the girl,
I wondered if she lived on common food.
One so ethereal, so angelical
Seemed far too near to heav'n, to be of earth.
I sometimes ventured to myself to say:
"She must have feasted on nectareous fruits,
Else whence the matchless bloom upon her face?
Or possibly of fragrant coffee sipped,
Or syllabub, or custard, or ice cream,
Or honey, or delicious patriots' food,
The rich baked sweet potatoes of our land."
When I first saw her at her father's house
Sit banqueting on common bread and meat,
And vegetables of the coarser sorts,
And learned she had an appetite for krout,
I was astonished, and could scarce believe
The testimony of my eyes and ears.
But it was fortunate for me and mine
That my good angel had warm, healthy blood,
Firm nerves, strong muscles, and most active limbs,
And worked untiringly in useful ways.

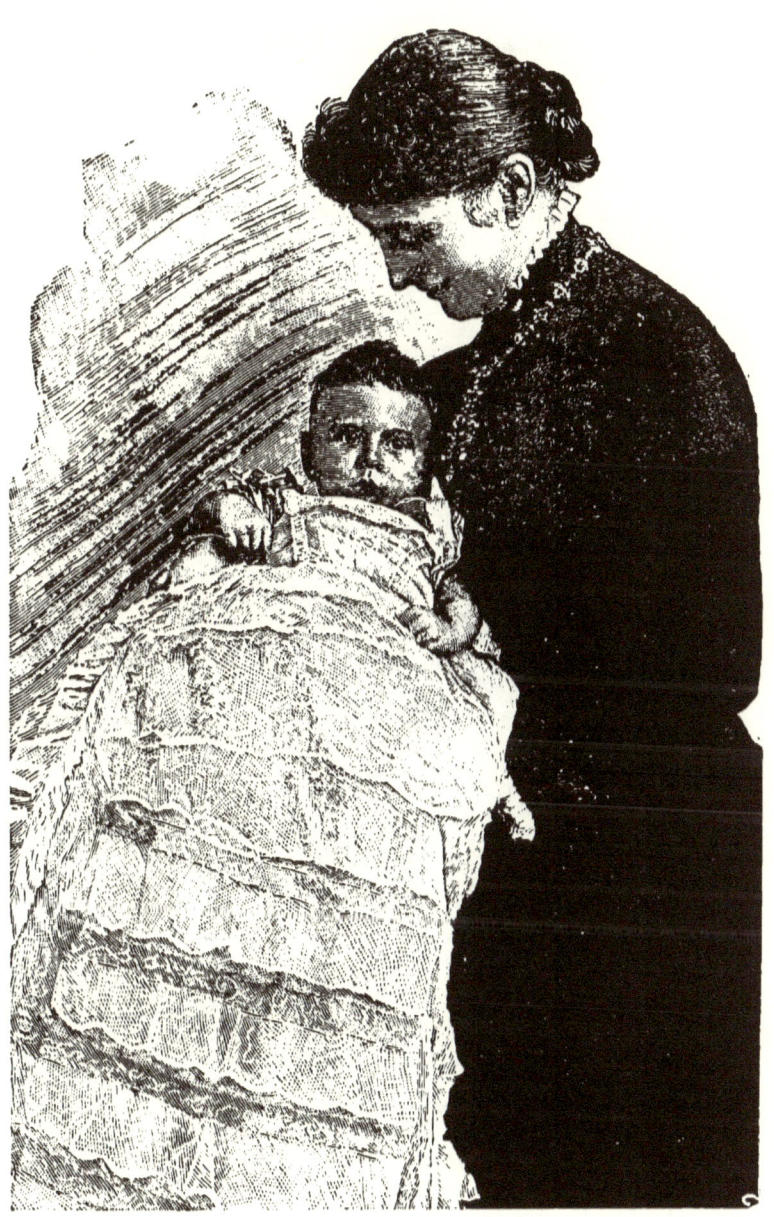

But it was fortunate for me and mine
That my good angel had warm, healthy blood.

Your eyes are asking if we ever wed.
Yes. 'Twas the most astounding mystery
Of all the num'rous myst'ries of my life
That she consented to become my own,
And link with loving courtesies her days
With my obscure and lowly destiny.

And worked untiringly in useful ways.

Near half a century of wedded bliss
Has proved how happily the poor may live.
Loves, births, and deaths have visited our house,
But hatreds have not dared to enter in.
Already half of our loved children stand
On the bright shores of immortality.

Their beck'ning hands invite us to the skies,
To share the glories of our upper home.
The guard and guide of my life's pilgrimage

Songs triumphant, jubilant, sublime.

Still gently leads us upward to our God;
And cheers the way with hopes and smiles and joys
And songs triumphant, jubilant, sublime.

THE BRIDAL MORN.

Yes, I ever shall remember
Those glad moments in September
When two hearts that love had captured
Saw a universe enraptured,
While all nature smiled delighted
On the vows that youth had plighted.
Even darkness seemed desiring,
Though at early dawn retiring,
To indulge in fond caressing
Or confer some priceless blessing
On the happy ones whose dreaming
With ecstatic bliss was teaming.
Starry hosts gazed fondly, brightly,
'Till Aurora, tripping lightly,
Passed the portals of the morning,
All the Orient adorning,
Then departed, gayly dancing,
As she saw the sun advancing;
But, obedient to duty,
Modest clouds, in dimpled beauty,
Came in rosy love tints flushing,
With admiring envy blushing,
Almost off'ring adoration
To the fairest of creation.
Misty morning stood enchanted
When his nimble feet were planted,
On the threshold where reclining
Loveliness was seen entwining
Op'ning buds and blooming flowers
For her happy nuptial hours.
Then the king of day came rushing,
Gloom and twilight swiftly brushing
From his pathway bright, and blazing;
While the world was wildly gazing
At the jewels which he lavished
On the hearts his grandeur ravished
When the radiant glory gleaming
From his face, with brightness beaming,
Blazed on river, lake, and fountain,

(30)

Flashed on valley, plain, and mountain,
Changing tear drops of the dawning
Into diamonds of the morning.
Round his steps were flowers blooming,
All the air with sweets perfuming,
While the blessèdness of heaven
Seemed to mortals richly given,
As on the bridal beauty glancing,
All was dazzling and entrancing.
Then the sportive hours stepped sprightly
As they saw their monarch lightly
Move in majesty and beauty
To perform his loving duty,
Nuptial torches gladly bearing,
As if more than honored sharing,
In the blissfulness attending
On the bridal that was blending
Hearts that death can never sever,
As they'll still love on forever,
In the home of love immortal
Just beyond the pearly portal.

VIRGINIA VISITED.

(32)

SELECTED POEMS.

VIRGINIA VISITED.

RICHMOND, VA., MAY, 1888.

HERE, loveliest of mothers,
　At home, from sorrows free,
I leave all else to others;
　And in my childish glee,
Entranced by charms that grace thee
　I stand beside thy knee;
Thy loving arms embrace me,
　While thrilling ecstasy
Bids care and gloom and sadness
　With quick'ning speed depart,
As in this hour of gladness
　I nestle near thy heart;
And lay my flushed cheek lightly
　Upon thy tender breast,
Where in my childhood nightly,
　I dreamed of heav'nly rest.

Through years of weary wand'ring,
　I've languished for thy smile,
My spirit fondly pond'ring,
　On ev'ry winning wile
That won my love, and bound me
　With fascinating pow'r,
And twined my heartstrings round thee,
　In childhood's guileless hour.
That sacred tie, unbroken,
　Still draws me to thy side,
With many a wish unspoken,
　That here I might abide.

3 　　　　　　　　　　　(33)

A dreary road, and lonely,
  I'll tread when we must part,
Though I have brought thee only
  A loving, homesick heart.

O best beloved of mothers!
  The "Iliad of thy woes"
Wrings from my noble brothers,
  And even from thy foes,
The bitter tears of sorrow
  And sympathetic grief,
That seek from God to borrow,
  For virtue, sweet relief.
'Twas when thy homes were blazing,
  By vandal fires consumed,
Th' indignant world stood gazing,
  And saw thy face illumed
With more than earthly glory;
  And thy majestic form,
Though battle-scarred and gory,
  Rose grandly through the storm.

Thermopylæs a hundred,
  And Marathons by scores,
Still tell where cannons thundered
  To guard thy sacred shores.
Yet not from puny Persians,
  Thy bloody fields were won,
Nor troops whose brief incursions
  End with the rising sun;
But men thou wouldst have cherished
  Were fiercest of thy foes,
And when they bravely perished,
  In agonizing throes,
Thou laidst their countless numbers
  Beside thy boldest braves,
To peaceful, quiet slumbers,
  In "hospitable graves."

O mother of the mighty!
  Thy matchless, gallant sons

Take precedence, and rightly,
  Of all earth's valiant ones;
Not Cæsar, nor Napoleon,
  Nor he of Macedon,
Nor German, Frank, nor Briton
  Could do what they have done.
The fabled hosts that Homer
  Made high Olympus tread
Were dwarfed beside each roamer
  That "Stonewall" Jackson led;
No gods of Grecian story
  Could bear comparison,
On fields of martial glory,
  With Lee or Washington.

By old Britannia's charter,
  A continent was thine;
Hills, plains, and sparkling water,
  Each forest and each mine.
The silv'ry voice of science
  Still pleads thy rightful claim,
And boldly bids defiance
  To all who scorn thy name,
"Virginiensis," brightly
  Her jeweled hand engraves
On birds that carol lightly,
  On tenants of the waves;
Fair flow'rets breathe it sweetly,
  It flashes on the tide,
The wild deer bears it fleetly
  Far up the mountain side.

Thy name, beloved, immortal
  Shall live when others die,
And to thy glowing portal
  Thy children ever hie.
When Time his course is ending,
  When all his works shall cease,
All eyes shall see, descending,
  The glorious Prince of Peace;
Then coming down from heaven,
  Christ's Virgin Bride shall shine,

Fair, sinless, pure, forgiven,
  Illustrious, divine!
And thou and thine shall with them
  Be blessed and satisfied,
As in the New Jerusalem,
  Virginia's glorified.

I'LL THINK OF THE SAND BANKS.*

LEXINGTON, KY., APRIL, 1839.

I'LL think of the sand banks when morn's early beam
Illumines the meadow and brightens the stream,
When noon's sultry sunshine invites to repose,
When night spreads oblivion o'er pleasures and woes;
E'en my dreams shall be peopled with forms that were
  there,
And their voices shall echo in fancy's rapt ear.

I'll think of the sand banks when spring paints her
  flow'rs
And calls her winged minstrels to gladden her bow'rs,
When summer's warm smile glows above the parched
  soil,
When autumn's rich stores bless the husbandman's toil,
And the chill winds of winter shall bring to my mind
The mem'ry of friends whom I there left behind.

I'll think of the sand banks while youth's eager eye
Still rests on hope's bow in futurity's sky;
When manhood with cares shall encircle my feet,
Or leave me, unfriended, life's troubles to meet;
And when age bids me gaze in the mirror of truth,
I'll think of the sand banks, the home of my youth.

TO MY MOTHER.†

I LOVE the land that gave me birth,
  The fires that warm my native hearth,

---

* Accomac, Va.
† Written at John Prather's, six miles East of Lexington, Ky.,
in the spring of 1842, and published in the *Ladies' Repository,*
Cincinnati, O.

I'll think of the sand banks when spring paints her flowers
And calls her winged minstrels to gladden her bowers.

(37)

The fields where childhood's sunny hours
Mid rip'ning fruits and op'ning flowers
Breathed pleasure in the floating air,
Nor thought of pain nor dreamed of care.

I love the home of infancy,
Virginia's charming scenery,
The sand banks of my native shore,
The whistling winds, the ocean's roar,
The storm careering fearfully,
The snow-capped surges wild and free.

I love the friends of early years,
Who kindly wiped my infant tears,
The humble church without a spire,
Where blazed devotion's hallowed fire,
The ministers of sacred truth
Who chid the wand'rings of my youth:

I love them all—God bless my home—
And shall where'er my steps may roam.
But, mother, when compared with thee,
To me they're less than vanity;
Next to the God she loves so well,
My mother in my heart shall dwell.

To guard my unprotected hours,
To strew my ev'ry path with flow'rs,
To make my childhood's sky grow bright,
To quell my fears was thy delight;
And with a love almost divine
Thine eyes grew dim in watching mine.

Dear mother, in my boyish dreams,
When fancy ruled her magic realms,
I gathered wealth that thy free hand
Might scatter blessings through the land,
I climbed Parnassian hills for fame,
To give thy house a deathless name.

I sought for honor's thorny road,
To mingle with the giddy crowd;
And when the rosy wreath was gained,

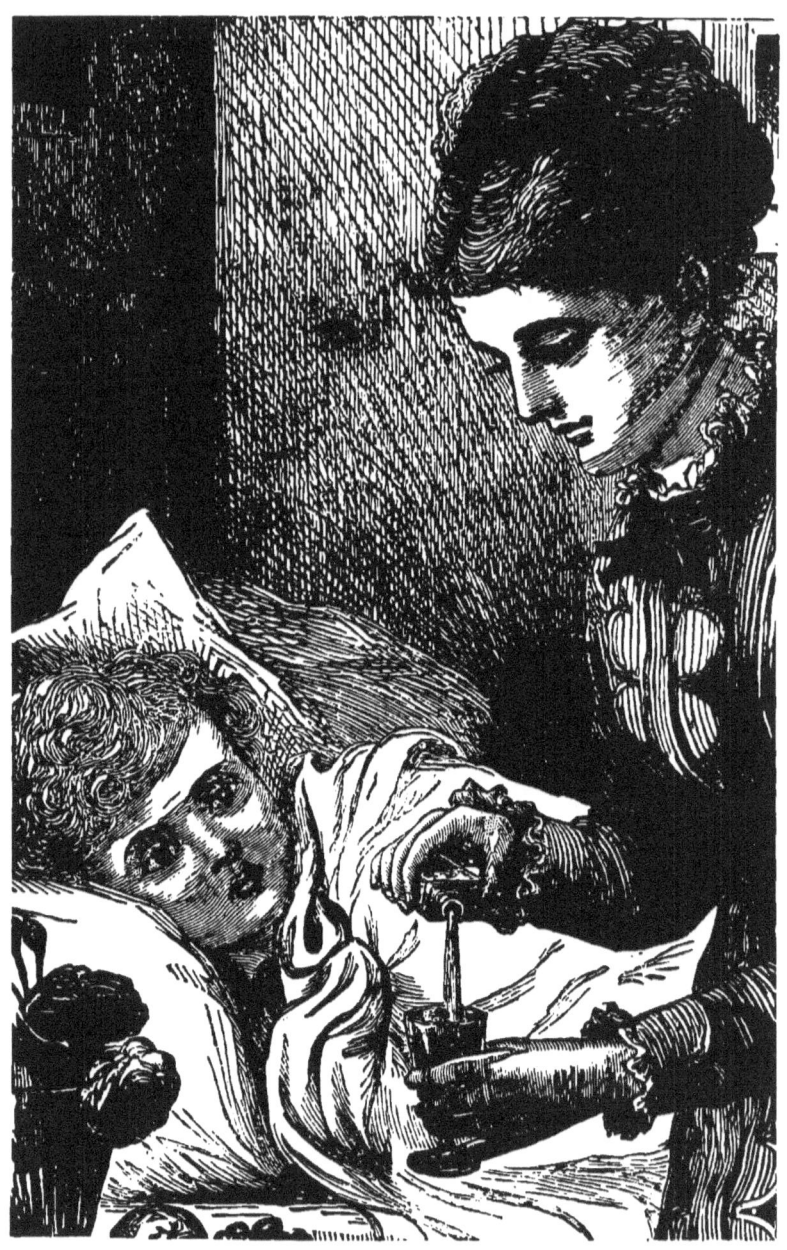

And with a love almost divine
Thine eyes grew dim in watching mine.

(39)

The sand banks of my native shore. The storm careering fearfully.
The whistling winds, the ocean's } The snow-capped surges wild and
roar, } free.

(40)

Though toil and blood its leaves had stained,
Delighted, at thy feet I'd bow,
And with it deck thy honored brow.

Those dreams have passed, and hopes of heav'n
To nobler themes my thoughts have giv'n;
Wealth's golden stores may ne'er be mine,
Nor fame my humble name enshrine.
The pathway of humility
Must lead my footsteps to the sky.

But, mother, when my wand'rings end
Where tall archangels lowly bend,
Joyful, their sovereign Lord to own,
And worship him who fills the throne;
Should Jesus deign to smile on me,
My thoughts shall fondly turn to thee.

And should a heav'nly harp be mine,
A crown of righteousness divine,
A mansion in the land of love,
A home in that bright world above,
'Twill sweeten all the joys of heaven
To know they're to my mother given.

A WIFE'S FIFTIETH BIRTHDAY.

JEFFERSONVILLE, IND., APRIL 20, 1873.

SINCE first I saw thee, thou hast ever been
My bright ideal of the beautiful,
The type and pattern of all loveliness.

Whether in gleeful gambolings, tripping
O'er flow'ry paths, where pleasure led the way,
In youth's bright morn; or at the noon of life,
Attending on love's myriad ministries
With steady step; or trudging cheerfully,
In later hours, o'er rough and rugged roads,
Where stern domestic drudg'ry drives her slaves—
Love's partial eye has seen in all thy steps
The poetry of motion and of grace.

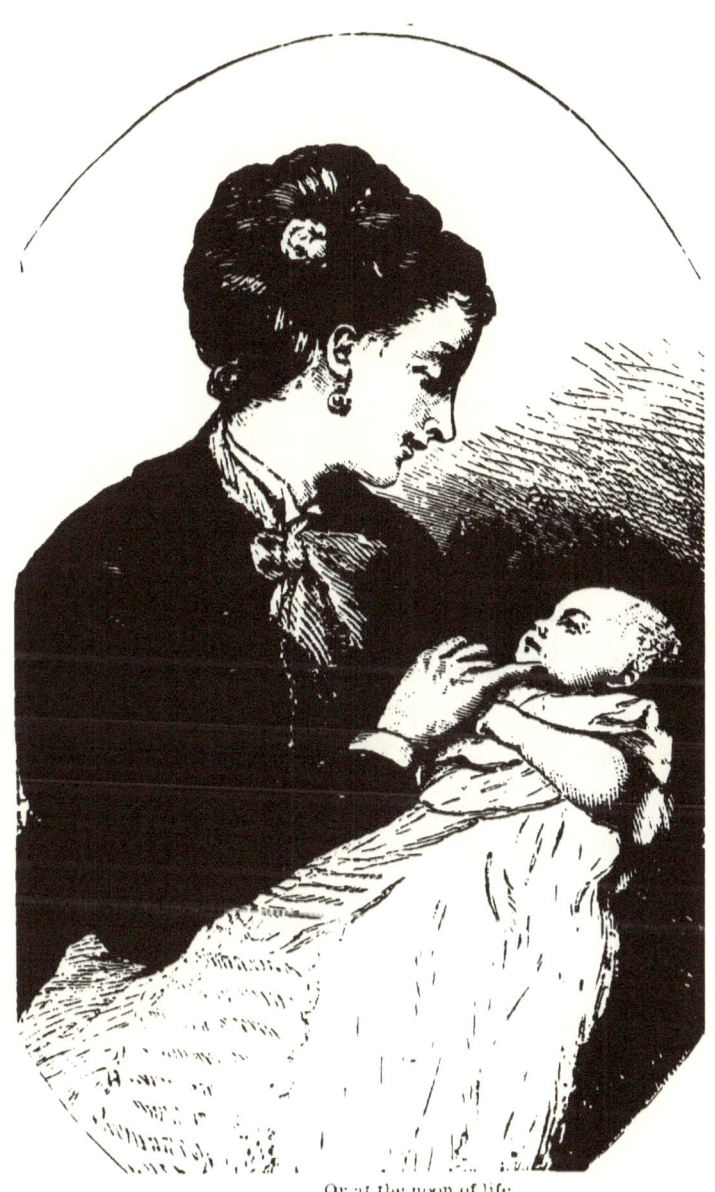

Or at the noon of life
Attend on love's myriad ministries.

(42)

Through all these happy hours thy gentle voice
Has seemed to pour upon my ravished ear
The music of that heav'n to which we go.
No weight of years has bent thy graceful form;
No sorrow dimmed the love light of thine eye;
The rose of beauty blooms upon thy cheek,
Still fadeless through the frosts of fifty years.
The hearts that long have gladdened in thy smile
Now gather round to hail thy natal hour.
So in the time to come this joyous day,
The brightest in the calendar, shall find
Thy throne of love, amid thy family,
In home's delightful summer land of bliss.

A TRUTHFUL IDYL OF REST AND RAPTURE.

ORLANDO, FLA., SEPTEMBER 4, 1888.

LET the bright needle rest to-day;
Books, pens, and work are laid away;
No toilsome thought shall hither stray;
The sportive sunbeams idly play
On the full ears of perfect corn,
That fertile, restful fields adorn.
They gayly dance and brightly smile
On many a lonely tropic isle;
Their languor-laden glory shines
Where ocean lazily reclines
In his broad bed at perfect ease,
And bids his slow-paced wavelets tease
The shy and modest slumb'rous shore
With their unceasing, sullen roar.
This sluggish air is not inclined
The paths of busy trade to find;
The soft-winged angels of repose
Float lightly on each breeze that blows.
Those grand old trees that, tow'ring high,
Rest their tall heads against the sky
Have done their work—borne buds and flow'rs
And rich, ripe fruit—in former hours.
The birds sit silent on the spray;

Their tender fledgelings, flown away,
Have left no chirping nursling brood,
With hungry cries demanding food.
In patriarchal grace and pride,
They're quiet, grave, and dignified.

Our tuneful offspring, loved and blest,
Have long since left the parent nest;
The children's children blithely play
Through all this fair September day.

Give me the hand that holds the thread,
The hand I long have gently led.
In loving clasp it still must stay;
Let the bright needle rest to-day.

Hold there! With speed old cares depart;
The warm pulsations of the heart
Rejuvenate the blood of age,
And all the faculties engage
To quicken life's slow, latent springs,
And give to fancy youthful wings.
Th' ecstatic, dear, delightful dream
Turns time's old turbid tide upstream:
Threescore and ten goes hobbling off;
See twenty-five his chapeau doff,
And gently bow his gallant form,
In heartfelt homage, high and warm,
Where graceful sixty-six resumes
The beauty that at twenty blooms.

Come to the parlor; take the arm
That still protects and shields from harm.
Tread lightly ou the hopes and fears
Of four and forty wedded years,
Whose blissful hours come smiling here,
To fill our hearts with lofty cheer.
Sing softly songs of former times:
There's rapture in their simple rhymes.
Let the old tunes that charm the soul
Sublimely swell and sweetly roll.

In this piano-prison bound
There's many a captive thrilling sound.
In harmony they all agree,
And wait your touch to set them free.
Though now their vocal chords are mute,
You'll find a remedy to suit;
The life of music lingers still
In fingers that, with magic skill,
Can draw from each obedient key
Sweet, soul-entrancing melody.

That heav'nly strain repeat, prolong:
An angel well might hush his song,
To pour upon his ravished ear
The rich, mellifluous sounds I hear.

We're young again, my precious bride;
And I, enraptured by thy side,
Recall the loveliness and grace
Of faultless form and matchless face
That won the heart that still is thine
And still delights to call thee mine.

THE FASTING, PRAYING CHURCH.

Written in Louisville, May, 1844, on the day set apart for prayer by the
General Conference on motion of Dr. John P. Durbin. Published in the
Ladies' Repository, Cincinnati, O.; copied by Dr. Thomas E. Bond, Sr.,
in *New York Advocate.*

CHURCH of my early choice, thy sons
    Are bathed in sorrow and in tears,
A company of sighing ones,
    A band of weeping worshipers;
Youth lays its joyousness aside;
    Age bends beneath its weight of care;
Beauty and strength forget their pride—
    All bow submissively in prayer.
And shall the suppliants depart
    In sadness from a throne of grace?
Shall quiv'ring lip and throbbing heart,
    Despairing, leave the sacred place?
O can the bruisèd, bending reed
    Be broken by the God of love?

No, Jesus lives to intercede;
    Thy living Head still reigns above.

Church of the living God, to thee
    A nation turns with anxious eye ;
Gloom gathers o'er thy destiny,
    And darkness spreads along thy sky;
Yet shall the storm cloud pass away,
    The lurid lightning cease to blaze;
The sunshine of a brighter day
    Shall gild thee with its gladd'ning rays.
E'en though thy legions should divide,
    One standard of the cross would wave,
One leader in thy front would ride,
    Mighty to conquer, strong to save.
Th' eternal God thy refuge is,
    The everlasting arms are thrown
Around the subjects of his grace,
    And he will safely keep his own.

Church of the poor, no creed of thine
    Has taught thy sons exclusiveness ;
They never claimed a right divine
    To curse the souls they could not bless;
To fetter thought or chain the mind;
    They ne'er have moved the civil pow'r.
Nor with the foes of man combined
    To lengthen out oppression's hour ;
No widow's tear, no orphan's sigh,
    No ashes of the martyred dead,
No cries of sainted souls on high
    Have called for vengeance on thy head.
But glad for thee the wilderness
    Now echoes to thy cheerful voice;
Cursed by the world, 'tis thine to bless
    Earth's erring sons with heav'nly joys.

Church of our fathers, 'tis thy hand
    Shall guide their offspring to the skies ;
While through thy courts, from ev'ry land,
    The hosts of the redeemed shall rise.

While wand'ring o'er his native sands,
   Or through the world in slav'ry driv'n,
The Ethiop, with outstretched hands,
   Shall seek through thee for rest in heav'n.
The Indian shall forget to roam,
   The war songs of the West shall cease,
And tenants of each wigwam home
   Be subjects of the Prince of Peace.
Through thee the Lord of hosts shall claim
   The distant nations for his own,
Till tribes of ev'ry tongue and name
   Fall worshiping before his throne.

VIRGINIA'S EASTERN SHORE, THE BRIDE OF OCEAN.

To My Grandson.

WHEN the great Genoese found a new world,
And laid its priceless treasures at the feet
Of Isabella, his fair patroness,
Rome's proud, presumptuous pontiff with vain words
Confirmed to her and hers the gen'rous gift;
But our proud island ancestors laid claim
To no small share of this rich heritage.
Cabot and Henry, Raleigh and Queen Bess,
And that John Smith whose manly majesty
Charmed Powhatan's loved daughter, wise Chatham,
Valiant Wolfe—all nobly toiled for England.
When the young giant of the West arose,
He drove out all intruders from his home, ·
His statesmen and his soldiers looked afar
Like Abraham when he beheld the realms
That God had given to his promised seed.
The prospect charmed them, and on battlefields
They severed all the ties that bound their lands
In subjugation base to foreign foes.
Wise statesmen and brave soldiers shall not fail
Till freedom's flag beneficently floats
O'er all the smiling fields and wat'ry wastes
From the Atlantic's central storm-tossed wave
To the far distant verdant isles that gem
Pacific's heaving bosom.   Nowhere else

THE GREATEST OF JOHN SMITHS.

(48)

He bids his waves
Pay homage at her feet.

4

In all this hemisphere is seen displayed
Such matchless beauty as old ocean weds.
Here in this "land of ev'ry land the pride"
He holds her to his palpitating heart
In chaste embrace, gently and tenderly
Laying around her his great loving arm;

FORTRESS MONROE.

The Chesapeake, bedecked with emeralds
And sparkling brightly with the dazzling blaze
Of waving diamonds, flashing back the light
Of sunbeams such as gild no other spot.

Embowered here amid earth's fairest flowers,
The great majestic main enamored rests,
Inhaling fragrance on each breeze that blows.
Delightful dalliance speeds the happy hours,
Adding new loveliness to dimpling smiles
And fascinating pow'r to ev'ry blush,
To each enchanting movement peerless grace,
Till in ecstatic bliss he bids his waves
Pay homage at her feet, and makes the earth,
The waters, and the air bring grandest gifts
To lavish on the object of his love.
In this unequaled home of ocean's bride
Six generations of your ancestors
Have lived, have loved, have worshiped, and been blest.

SUNRISE AT THE FALLS OF THE OHIO.

Respectfully Inscribed to My Artist Friend, J. W. C.

'Twas in my daydream's fantasy
  Wealth, happiness, and fame
Crowned one who wears most worthily
  An honored father's name.
He left his downy couch at dawn
  To sketch a sunrise view,
And by the misty light of morn
  Its shad'wy outlines drew,
As, standing on a lofty height,
  A maiden by his side
Filled playful children with delight
  All garlanded in pride.
Then tenants of the pasture came
  To greet their human friends,
Each with an honest, rightful claim
  To gifts our Father sends.
The little ones right merrily
  Their fleecy guests embraced;
Round pony's neck in girlish glee
  The maiden's arms were placed.
The artist from his easel turned
  To see the petted brute,

That glowing flush illumed the floods,
The valleys, and the plains.

(52)

Yet, though his heart with envy burned,
  His tongue and lips were mute;
For through the morning mists afar
  He saw the grass-grown hills
That, ere an elemental war
  Had freed th' imprisoned rills,
Inclosed a prehistoric lake
  With beauteous isles bedecked;
But Titan hands with rending quake
  Had Muldrough's mountain wrecked,
Dug out a channel for the streams,
  And set the waters free
To sparkle in the sun's bright beams,
  Unfettered toward the sea.
He gazed until the sky had smiled
  Away its look of gloom,
And blushed with beauty that beguiled
  Dull darkness to his doom.
That glowing flush illumed the floods,
  The valleys, and the plains,
And waked the warblers of the woods
  To sing their sweetest strains;
Made iron tracks of commerce seem
  Like massive bars of gold,
O'er which with lightning's speed and gleam,
  Trade's thund'ring chariots rolled.
The bridges stretched their giant arms
  Across the shining stream,
Clothed in refulgent borrowed charms
  Lent by the early beam;
The grand canal reposed in pride,
  Within her marble walls,
And saw the fleets of commerce glide
  In grandeur round the falls.
Each rock shone like a radiant gem,
  Each wave seemed glitt'ring ore
Which formed a matchless diadem
  Kentucky proudly wore.
Her robe of emerald, bedecked
  With diamonds of dew,

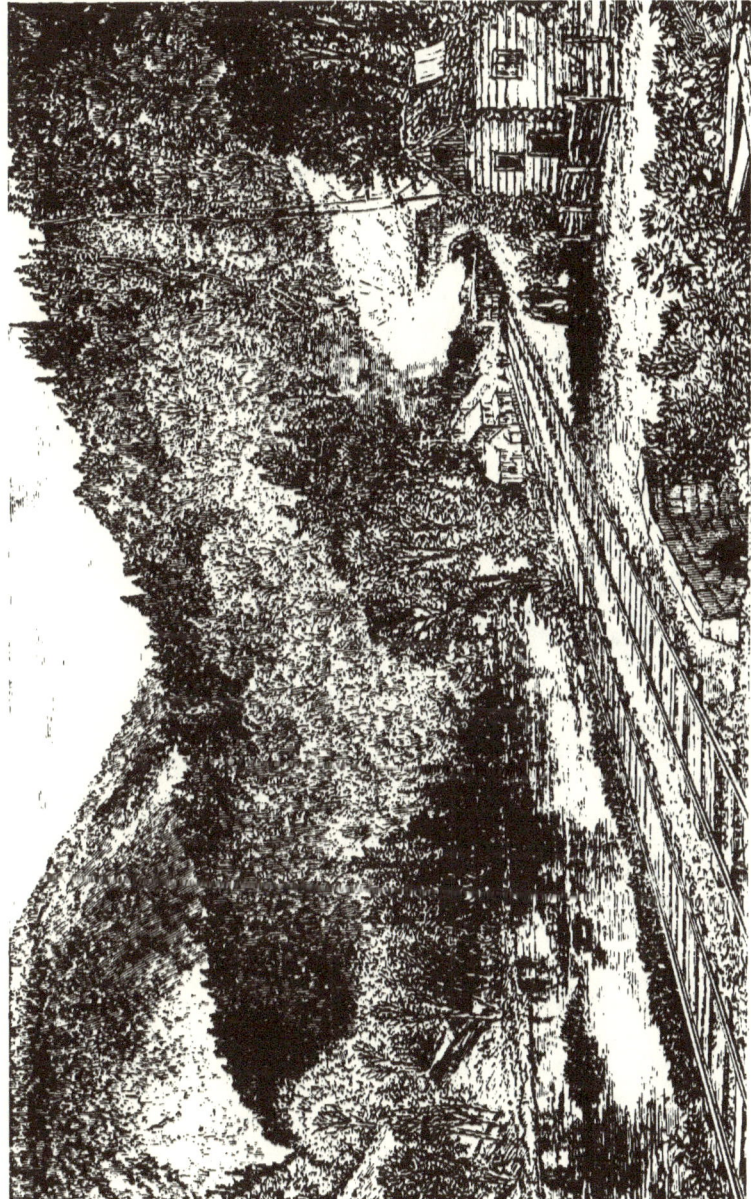

Made iron tracks of commerce seen
Like massive bars of gold.

(54)

Aurora's pencil faintly flecked
  With dyes of roseate hue.
In stately majesty and grace,
  Unseen on royal thrones,
With beauty's bloom upon her face,
  With music in her tones,
In loveliness she gayly roves,
  And fairer none can be
Except the mother that she loves,
  Who sits beside the sea,
Who glories in such gallant sons
  As Washington and Lee,
And all her other noble ones,
  Free leaders of the free.
So mused the artist as he gazed,
  Till on his dazzled sight
The sky, the earth, the waters blazed,
  With wondrous glory bright.
'Twas sunrise on the belching fires
  Of mammon at his feet,
And sunrise on the domes and spires
  Where saints delight to meet,
And where the sleepers are at rest
  In forty thousand homes
That shone like mansions of the blest,
  Where sorrow never comes.
'Twas sunrise on the maiden's brow,
  And in the painter's heart,
For he beheld a landscape now
  Full worthy of his art.
'Twas graven on his raptured soul,
  In all its gorgeous hues;
And under his complete control
  At will to reproduce.
He gave that sunrise scene to all,
  Of ev'ry age and clime,
And let its light descend and fall
  On all the tracts of time.
It led the patient painter's way
  To fortune and to fame,
Still flashing on the brow of day,
  His own illustrious name.

"THROUGH HIM WE BOTH HAVE ACCESS BY ONE SPIRIT UNTO THE FATHER."

PART FIRST.

ETERNAL, self-existent Lord,
  In thee alone was life or power,
Till thy omnific, sovereign Word
  Flashed light on nature's natal hour.

The glorious universe complete,
  From thy exhaustless fullness came,
With grandeur, beauty, love replete,
  Thy wondrous glories to proclaim.

Father of all, in all thou art;
  Immensity is filled with thee:
We cannot from thy sight depart,
  Nor from thy awful presence flee.

We would not Father, leave thy side,
  Or doubt thy all-abounding grace,
In thee we live, in thee confide,
  Yet cannot see thy glorious face;

But in thine own eternal Son
  The Godhead bodily appears,
At thy right hand, upon thy throne,
  Immanuel our nature wears.

In Him, almighty to redeem,
  The brightness of thy glory shines;
The image of thyself in him
  Expresses all thy kind designs.

Th' incarnate Son, for sinners slain,
  With matchless majesty and love,
Suffered and died, and rose again
  To plead for us in realms above.

PART SECOND.

High in the heavens our Saviour reigns,
  But can he on the earth be found,
To break the adamantine chains
  With which the sinner's soul is bound?

THE ASCENSION.

(57)

He comes not upward from the deep,
  Nor from the heights of glory down,
He shows not to the eyes that weep
  His starry or his thorny crown.

We cannot on his bosom rest,
  Nor with him for an hour abide,

THE TRANSFIGURATION.

Nor follow, at his own request,
  His footsteps up the mountain side.

Nor trembling touch with anxious fears,
  His garments on the crowded street
Or wash with penitential tears,
  The dust of travel from his feet;

Or catch the pitying look that broke
  Poor Peter's heart, with sacred grief;
Or hear the gentle voice that spoke
  The pardon to the dying thief.

Father, his body is not here,
  To give our souls access to thee,

WASHING FEET WITH TEARS.

To hush the sigh, to wipe the tear,
  That tells the heart's deep agony.

But in the storms of dire distress,
  That gloom the penitential hour,
He has not left us comfortless:
  We feel the Holy Spirit's power.

PART THIRD.

Sent from the Father, by the Son,
　The Holy Ghost, in person comes,
To comfort each believing one,
　And dwell within our humble homes.

THE CRUCIFIXION.

He leads us to the crimson flood,
　That ev'ry human soul redeemed,
Precious, propitiatory blood,
　That from the wounds of Jesus streamed.

Ho makes tho leprous sinner clean,
  Blots out the record of our shame,
Takes from us all the guilt of sin,
  And writes within us the new name.

Omnipotently strong to save,
  He ends the struggle and the strife;
He raised our Saviour from the grave,
  And gives dead souls eternal life.

In manifested pow'r and love
  He makes our bodies his abode,
And fleshly tabernacles prove
  The temples of the living God.

By him, through Jesus, we obtain
  Access to thee, and in thee live;
And with thee, Father, all things gain,
  That man can need or God can give.

The universe at thy command
  Lays its rich treasures at our feet,
And as we in thine image stand,
  Thy presence makes our bliss complete.

THE APOSTLES' CREED IN VERSE.

I BELIEVE in God the Father,
  The almighty, the divine,
Father of my Lord and Saviour,
  And, O blessèd thought! he's mine.
I believe in God the Father;
  Not in chance nor gloomy fate:
That 'twas he with wond'rous wisdom
  Did the universe create:
That he made the earth and heav'ns
  For the children of his love,
And intends that they shall ever
  Dwell in bliss with him above.

He is my own loving Father,
    No poor orphan waif am I;
I'm an heir of endless glory,
    I'm a child of the Most High.

I believe in our Lord Jesus,
    The divine, anointed One;

Born of blessed Virgin Mary.

He alone is the Begotten,
    He is the Eternal Son.
Born of blessèd Virgin Mary,
    By the Holy Ghost conceived,
He was love divine, incarnate,
    Yet by men was not received.

That he, under Pontius Pilate,
    Suffered, bled, was crucified,
Bearing all our sins upon him,
    When in agony he died.

I believe his body buried
    Lay in Joseph's marble tomb
Till the third auspicious morning
    When he left it's dismal gloom:
Then o'er death and hell triumphant
    He ascended into heav'n,
At the right hand of the Father,
    Where to him all pow'r is giv'n.

On his great white throne descending,
    He will judge the quick and dead,
When the awe-struck earth and heavens
    From before his face have fled.

I adore thee, Lord and Saviour,
    For thou wast and art divine,
On the throne of Triune Godhead,
    Or in this poor heart of mine.
I adore thee in the myst'ry
    That incarnates deity,
In the judgment hall of Pilate,
    In expiring agony;
In thy vict'ry over Satan,
    Over death, hell, and the grave,
Giving perfect demonstration
    Of omnipotence to save.
I adore my Mediator
    In the heav'nly heights above,
On his awful throne of judgment,
    Which to me's a throne of love.
He will vindicate his people,
    Be thou jubilant, my soul!
Thou shalt reign in joyous rapture,
    While eternal ages roll.

In the Holy Ghost eternal,
    I with all my heart believe;

In his offices and person,
  His divinity receive.
I rely on him for comfort,
  And for freedom from all sin:
He will cleanse his human temple,
  And enshrine himself within.
'Tis by him that we have access
  To the Father, through the Son,
He will guide and help and strengthen,
  Till our work on earth is done.

In the Church of God believing,
  I would seek no hermit's cell;
Church on earth, and in the heavens
  Let me with your members dwell.

I believe in sweet communion
  With the saints of the Most High,
In their fellowship I'm living,
  And among them I shall die.
I believe in the remission
  And the blotting out of sins;
When, with faith in the Redeemer,
  Everlasting life begins;
Not to end when this poor body
  Heaves it's last expiring breath,
But exist in conscious glory,
  Endless ages after death.

In the body's resurrection
  I implicitly believe,
As the Lord descends from heaven,
  All his people to receive;
They, arising in his likeness,
  Shall be glorious like their Lord,
Incorruptible! immortal!
  And, according to his word,
Shall in joyous exultation
  And ecstatic rapture sing:
"Where, O grave, is now thy vict'ry?
  Where, O death, thy pointless sting?"

There's nothing
half so sweet in life as
LOVE'S YOUNG DREAM
except
THE HONEY-MOON
of one who has been a
widow or widower.